For Matt, Paul, Chad, Sorche, Lori,
my great family,
and, of course, Number Three,
whom I have been friends with my entire life

Henry Holt and Company, LLC
Publishers since 1866
175 Fifth Avenue
New York, New York 10010
mackids.com

Library of Congress Cataloging-in-Publication Data
Dernavich, Drew, author, illustrator.
It's not easy being Number Three / Drew Dernavich.—First edition.
pages   cm
Summary: Bored with doing the same thing all the time, Number Three quits and sets out to see
what else he might do, then, after trying many other possibilities, finally finds the perfect job.
ISBN 978-1-62779-208-0 (hardcover)
[1. Three (The number)—Fiction. 2. Contentment—Fiction.] I. Title. II. Title: It is not easy being Number Three.
PZ7.1.D475It 2016   [E]—dc23   2015004516

Henry Holt books may be purchased for business or promotional use. For information on
bulk purchases, please contact the Macmillan Corporate and Premium Sales Department
at (800) 221-7945 x5442 or by e-mail at specialmarkets@macmillan.com.

First Edition—2016 / Designed by April Ward
The artist used India ink on scratchboard and Adobe Photoshop to create the illustrations for this book.
Printed in China by Toppan Leefung Printing Ltd., Dongguan City, Guangdong Province

1 3 5 7 9 10 8 6 4 2

IT'S NOT EASY BEING NUMBER THREE

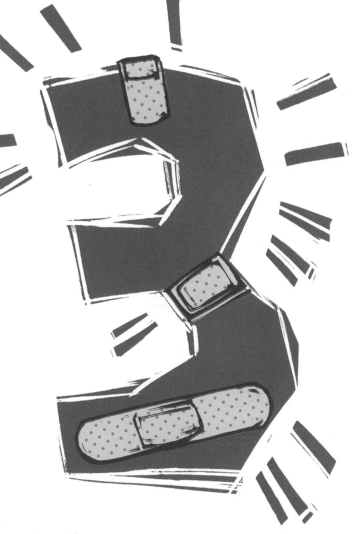

DREW DERNAVICH

Christy Ottaviano Books

Henry Holt and Company 🍎 New York

Do you know Number Three?
I mean, do you really *know* Number Three?

You might think you do. After all, numbers are everywhere.

But sometimes numbers get bored and want to do something else.

And they really wish they could just quit being a number for a while.

But what was a number supposed
to do once it stopped being a number?
There were so many possibilities,
so many things to try!

And Number Three wanted to try them all.

Could he be the toes
of an elephant?

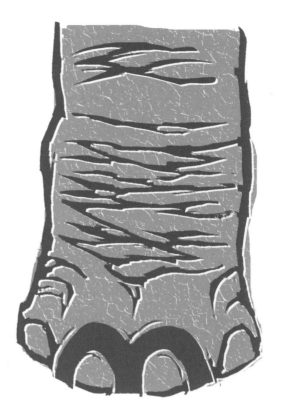

The mouth of a cat?

The humps of a camel?

The wings of a seagull?

Number Three liked people even more than he liked animals, so he tried being

the rim of some glasses,

the legs on a pair of shorts,

and an earbud.

He also tried being a shoelace,

the hem of a dress,

and even a hair band.

But none of those options felt satisfying. Number Three soon found himself sitting in the laundry basket, feeling unappreciated.

Maybe he could do something helpful, like work in a school.
There were so many useful things he could be in a classroom.

But he didn't enjoy the nights and weekends when kids weren't around. There was nobody for him to help, and that left Three feeling lonely.

Wasn't there something more active that Number Three could do?

Like being a rake in a big backyard?

A ship's anchor, plunging into the ocean?

A spatula in a busy restaurant?

The steering wheel of an airplane?

These things were certainly exciting, but they left Number Three a little banged up.

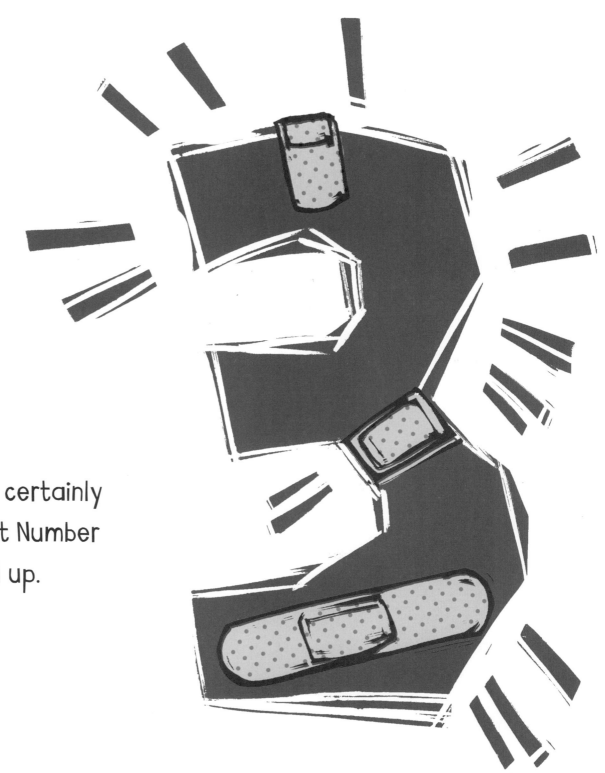

That was when Number Three decided to be a sculpture.
Everybody would see him, and he wouldn't get hurt.
Now this was fun! He had a shiny coat of bronze and
a pedestal to sit on. People said he was a work of art!
Number Three was making people happy, so he felt happy.

The other numbers heard about Number Three's new job and came by to say hello.

But Number Three wasn't interested in returning to the world of numbers.

Everybody appreciates me. I've never felt so important! Sorry, Numbers. You'll have to get along without me.

And so, Number Three continued to be a sculpture.

But as the days and weeks went on, he felt less and less special. Eventually, his shiny bronze coat got dull and dirty.

Very dirty.

Then winter came. People stopped gathering in front of
Number Three and taking pictures. He didn't feel so important
anymore. And he became more unhappy with each passing day.

Pretty soon, nobody noticed that Number Three was there at all. What could he do that would make him feel useful again?

When the snow started to melt, Number Three saw a glimmer of hope in a new sign: The State Fair would be coming this spring. Number Three loved the fair! He knew he had to go!

As soon as it was time, Number Three gladly hopped off his lonely pedestal.

C·L·O·T·H·E·S,
OBVIOUSLY

He rushed to find a disguise so that nobody would notice him . . .

and then he went off to enjoy the fair.

But when Number Three got there, he was shocked by what he saw. There was no fair this year!

"There's no three-legged race,

no three throws
for a dollar,

no triple-scoop
ice-cream cones,

no three times around on the Ferris wheel. . . .

A ONE, AND A TWO, AND A . . . AND A . . .

"We can't even
have music!

"What's worse, the other numbers couldn't take
Three's place, so they all had to quit.

"There are
no games

or prizes.

"There's no
way to even tell
the time or the
temperature!

"Without the numbers, there's no fun."
It didn't take Number Three long to realize
that this was the opportunity he was looking for.
He was going to be useful again, just by being
himself. And this made him feel like celebrating!